ease return this book to the
fore the last date stamped
letter, telephone or in pe
oks at the rate currently det

14 JUL 1998

-- NOV 2003

-- FEB 2005

REGIN, E.

he Magical Bicycle

THE
MAGICAL
BICYCLE

For Yvonne and Ezra with love
and gratitude.

THE MAGICAL BICYCLE

Elana Bregin

MAMMOTH

First published in Great Britain 1990
by William Heinemann Ltd
Published 1992 by Mammoth
an imprint of Mandarin Paperbacks
Michelin House, 81 Fulham Road, London SW3 6RB

Mandarin is an imprint of the Octopus Publishing Group,
a division of Reed International Books Limited

Copyright © 1990 Elana Bregin

ISBN 0 7497 0939 1

A CIP catalogue record for this title
is available from the British Library

Printed in Great Britain
by Cox & Wyman Ltd, Reading, Berkshire

To Zodwa Gubevu who taught me about Zulu people – *ungisizile*.

THE CITY OF BICYCLES

If there was one thing Thomas wanted more than anything in the world, it was a bicycle. He had dreamed of having a bicycle for as long as he could remember. But where was a boy like him to get such a thing?

In his family there were five children – himself and four younger girls. They stayed with their grandmother in the black township of Wozani, near to the big city of Silverton. Silverton was where their mother lived. She had work there in one of the white suburbs as a domestic servant – a good job, that paid better wages than most. But even so, with five children to feed and clothe, rent to pay and Thomas's schooling to see to, there wasn't anything over for luxuries like bicycles.

7

But that was often the way of things in Wozani. There were many other families there like Thomas's, with too many children and too little money. In his neighbourhood, where people often went hungry, one saw few bicycles. And those belonged not to children, but grown men. Mostly, they were old machines, cumbersome and ugly. But Thomas's eyes fell upon them with wistful longing.

He would have given anything for the chance to ride one himself, to sit like a king above the world and be carried away by the spinning wheels; to glide like a hawk past the plodders on foot.

But such delights were not for children like him to know. If he wanted a bicycle, his grandmother had told him, he would have to wait. When he was older and working and earning money of his own, he could buy one for himself. Till then, he would have to be patient.

To Thomas, it seemed that not all the patience in Wozani would be enough to see him through so many years of waiting. Every bicycle that went by took a little piece of his heart away with it.

Only his favourite sister, Thandi, knew

the extent of his longing. 'Maybe you will get some good fortune,' she would try to comfort him. 'Maybe you will find a rich person who likes you and will buy you your own bicycle.'

But even as a daydream, her words sounded far-fetched. Thomas didn't know any rich people. All the people he saw in Wozani were as poor as himself.

That was before he came to Silverton, to the white suburb of plenty. People there were rich; at first, Thomas couldn't believe how rich. In their houses, not even the dogs went hungry. Motor cars were parked in spaces where whole families could have lived. And bicycles were as common as trees.

Thomas had come to Silverton at the start of the summer holidays, to stay with his mother until the schools re-opened in the New Year. She had asked special permission from her Madam to have him with her. She didn't want him in the township over Christmas time, with all the bad things that were happening there at present. She was afraid that with no school to keep him off the streets, he would get into trouble.

And undoubtedly, she was right. You

didn't have to go looking for trouble in the townships these days. It had a habit of coming to find you, whether you wanted it or not. It was different for his sisters. They were girls, and too small to bother with anyway. But Thomas was ten. And that was a dangerous age to be, in these times of confusion.

Ten was old enough to be shot at by police or army, if you should happen to be in a place where trouble broke out. Ten was also old enough to draw the attention of those calling themselves 'Comrades'.

Gangs of them frequently roamed the streets, looking for boys like Thomas, whom they could persuade to join the struggle. They said the townships were at war. Exactly with whom, or why, Thomas never really understood, but he knew it had something to do with Freedom. And if some of these Comrades spotted you, and invited you to join them in some stone-throwing or slogan-shouting or tyre-burning to prove your support for the struggle, it was better not to refuse. If you refused you showed yourself not to be with the people at all, but an enemy. And there wasn't a boy in Wozani who didn't understand what *that* meant.

No, Thomas was not sorry to leave the turmoil of the township behind him for a while and join his mother in peaceful Silverton. Silverton was a different world altogether. Here, there was no war. There were no Comrades, no army, no teargas, no roaring, angry mobs. No smell of burning rubber, or cries and screams in the night.

Life here was tree-lined streets and swimming pools; big houses, smart cars, servants, TVs and . . . bicycles. Bicycles by the dozen, whizzing by with a sound like hornets, jostling on the pavements, racing neck and neck along the smooth-tarred roads. Not old and battered bicycles, like the ones he saw in Wozani, but brand, shining new; with gleaming chrome colours and glittery writing on the frames, with fancy handlebars and special gears. They made Thomas's heart burn with helpless envy.

In his badly-fitting red shorts and Mr T sweat-shirt that the kind Madam had donated, Thomas would stand against the wall at the bottom of the driveway, and watch the bicycles at play.

The street where his mother's Madam

lived was the perfect haunt for bicycles. It was long and broad and shady, with just the right amount of slope in its centre; and being a cul-de-sac, it didn't get much traffic.

A group of children from the neighbourhood met regularly there in the holidays, and spent a lot of time riding up and down, inventing new games, having races – and generally annoying the residents with their yells and racket. But Thomas found them great fun to watch.

They tied home-made wooden carts to the backs of their bicycles and took turns pulling each other up and down. They loaded their water pistols, and their catapults with paper pellets, and fought noisy 'cavalry' battles in the street. They had relays and 'handicap' races, and tried to outdo each other with tricks and stunts. They ramp-jumped over sand-mounds and set up obstacle courses with old tyres and planks and ropes and beer-cans.

They always seemed to be having the greatest fun. Thomas would look on wistfully from his place in the driveway, longing to join in, hoping against hope that someone would offer him a turn on a bike. But no one ever did.

The boy whom he liked best out of all the group was the one the others called Kevin – a cheerful, lanky-limbed boy with front teeth like a rabbit's and merry green eyes.

Kevin wasn't the oldest in the group, or the biggest, or the one with the best bike. But it was easy to see that he was the one they all looked up to. It was he who thought up the games, who decided the rules, who settled the arguments. In anything to do with bicycles, he was the champion. He could race faster, ramp-jump higher, balance better than anyone else in the group. And he was a real daredevil; the more difficult and dangerous a challenge was, the better he seemed to like it.

Thomas would watch with his heart in his mouth as the other boy went flying down the sloping street sitting backwards on the saddle; or tried to push himself up into a handstand on the handlebars, while the bike was in full motion; or wobbled across a ledge so narrow you just knew he had to fall.

He was always having to pay for his daring – always covered in bruises and grazes, with bleeding knees and scabby elbows. He fell off his bicycle so often he hardly even seemed to notice any more. He would just pick himself up, inspect himself absently for damage, and go right back to doing whatever he had been doing before.

Thomas admired him tremendously. Kevin was the only one of the group who ever took any notice of him. Sometimes, as he whizzed past and saw Thomas standing there, stuck to the wall like part of the brickwork, he would grin his cheeky grin, waggle two fingers above his head, and drawl out; '*Ma-a-gical*!'

Usually, Thomas was too shy to do more than grin back and squirm even deeper against the wall. But he liked very much to be greeted in this way; it made him feel part of the group.

That word 'magical' was one that the bicycle children used a lot. It was Kevin's favourite word. He never said 'Hello,' or 'Goodbye,' or 'How are you?' the way other people did. He never said something was nice, or clever, or a good idea; he just said, 'Ma-a-gical.'

He had his own way of saying the word, drawing out its syllables, that gave it a colour all of its own.

Thomas soon picked up the habit.

'Ma-a-gical,' he would murmur breathily, in just the tone Kevin used, when he saw a bicycle he admired. Or if one of the children did something that impressed him. And often, in the excitement of the bicycle games, he would find himself shouting it out loud. 'Magical!' he would whoop from his solitary corner, 'Magi-*cal*!' he would cry, as Kevin swooped past like a swallow, to win yet another race; or shot through the air in a ramp-jump so spectacular it took your breath away. And his voice would be swelled by other voices, by a chorus of 'Magi-cal!'s – all bursting out at the same moment, from a dozen excited throats at once.

Then, the word would seem to gain a special power. Thomas would feel lifted up by it, elated and thrilled; as if it was he who had won the race, or hovered there in space for timeless moments. Like a warm, friendly wave, the cry would break around him, sweeping him up out of his lonely corner and making him feel, for those brief seconds, part of the group.

Pleasant though Silverton was, there were often times during those early days when Thomas wished himself back in Wozani.

His mother, busy with her work in the big house, had little time to spare him, and he often felt lonely. He missed his grandmother and his sisters, particularly little Thandi; and he missed his playmates.

Here, he had no friends. The white children weren't used to playing with black boys. He wasn't from their world, and they didn't think of him as one of themselves, or as someone they could be friends with.

So much of the time, Thomas was left to his own company. He would amuse himself, when he wasn't watching the bicycle games, by making *Izinqola* – small toy cars and bicycles out of wire, to wheel around. Or else he would simply sit up on the shaded steps near the kia, where he stayed with his mother, daydreaming of bicycles.

Once or twice, he had been down to the nearby park, to play on the swings. He was allowed to do that now his mother's Madam had told him it was all right. In Silverton these days, the parks were all open to blacks. The 'Whites Only' signs had been taken down, and no one was allowed to chase him away.

But the white Madams who came to the swings with their children didn't like to find him there. They looked at him so crossly it made him uncomfortable. And once, one had even told him in a loud voice to 'Get away and play in your own parks!'

Since that happened, he hadn't been back. If he needed something to do, he preferred just to go wandering through the streets, where no one bothered him; admiring the handsome houses with their flower-filled gardens, and wishing Thandi could be there to see them too.

THE OLD GRANDMOTHER IN THE LOT

There was, in that neighbourhood, not far from the house where Thomas's mother worked, a certain street where white children had been warned by their parents never to walk after dark.

At the far end of this street, adjoining the last house, was an empty piece of ground – a big open lot, all overgrown with weeds and grass and tangles, its far end shadowed by the creeping bush that invaded it from the hillside behind. It was where people came and dumped their garden rubbish. There were bricks and bottles scattered about, the shell of a car, and strips of corrugated sheeting from the collapsing fence that half-divided the lot from the road.

No one knew to whom the piece of

ground belonged. It had stood empty since the neighbourhood began. Over the years, it had become a haven for tramps and drunks and squatters, for all the sad, homeless people who didn't have anywhere else to go. They slept in the cover of the bushes, sometimes making themselves crude shelters out of cardboard or fence-sheeting or whatever else they could find to nail or tie together.

The white people were always complaining about the lot, calling it 'an eyesore' and 'a disgrace.' They were always badgering the local authorities to 'do something about it.'

Every so often, the police vans would come by; the shelters in the bushes would be torn down, the vagrants herded up and carted away. And for a brief while, the lot would be almost respectable again. But it never took long before it started filling once more. New homeless people would arrive, drifting in from nowhere like tumbleweed in the wind. And in no time, the shanties would be sprouting, there would be fires smoking, bottles clinking, drunken voices echoing in the night. And the phones in the Complaints Office of the police station would start ringing all over again.

Among the ever-changing residents who came and went amid the weeds and shadows, was one who had made the lot her permanent home. She was an old, coffee-coloured woman, wrinkled now, but with traces still of a fine, proud beauty. Her cheekbones were high and slanted, her nose hawkish, and her eyes snapped like black lightning.

In her, was a mix of many races. Even the most determined official of Race Class-ification would find it hard to unravel her complicated ancestry. For she was Xhosa and Zulu, Hottentot and Indian, Huguenot and Dutch.

Where she had come from, nobody knew, but she had been part of the lot for as long as anybody could remember. The local black people feared and respected her. They brought her gifts of food and blankets, and sought her advice. And they took great care not to offend her or cross her will. For there were many rumours told about this Old One.

It was whispered that in former days, she had been a Sorceress, that she had Powers, that she could work strange magic. Whether or not such rumours were true, no one could say for sure. But it was a funny thing how, whenever the police vans arrived to do their duty and make the lot respectable again, it never happened that this Old One was among the unfortunates they carted off. Even her shelter of wood and tin was never pulled down like the others were. True, it was well camouflaged in its overgrown corner deep in the bushes. But the black people swore there were other reasons why it wasn't touched.

Now it happened, one sunny morning, that Thomas was walking down this street where the lot was situated, guiding with one hand a small wire bicycle he had recently made, and holding in the other a nice thick, sticky slice of bread and jam. He was singing happily to himself as he padded along the pavement, eyeing his doorstep of bread and anticipating the moment when he would sink his strong, hungry teeth into its softness.

He had reached the edge of the fencing that enclosed the lot, and was just passing by the gap where a number of the sheets had fallen in, when he heard a voice hailing him. He stopped in surprise and looked behind him at the empty pavement. Then he ducked his head and peered through the fence into the lot.

A strange, sweet smell wafted up to him from the weedy shadows, but at first, he couldn't see anybody. Then his gaze slid lower, and he made out an old woman, sitting comfortably stretched out in the shade against one of the fence supports. She had a blanket of patterned wool draped across her body. Her head was wrapped in a turban of bright silk cloth, and in her teeth, she held a long-stemmed wooden Xhosa pipe, from which the sweet-smelling puffs of smoke were steadily rising.

Thomas, being a stranger to the area, didn't know the rumours. No one had mentioned to him anything about the 'Sorceress' in the lot. All he saw when he looked at her was an old brown woman of uncertain race, warming her aged bones in the sunshine. Yet there was something in her face that wasn't old. Even in the shadows, her black eyes glittered with strange power. When they fastened themselves on Thomas's face, he found he wanted to look away. But she was beckoning him closer; so he picked up his wire toy, balanced his slice of breakfast on his palm and stooped through the fence.

'I see you, Grandmother,' he muttered respectfully, in answer to her own greeting. 'How are you?'

'Not well, my son, not well,' came the reply. 'Age makes my bones ache. Not even the sun can warm the stiffness from them anymore.' Thomas nodded sympathetically. He knew too well from his own grandmother, about the pains of growing old.

'And what is more,' the Old One continued, 'I am very hungry. Give me some of your bread.'

'This bread, Grandmother?' Thomas's fingers tightened on his portion in dismay.

'I see no other, my son.' The dark eyes, steady on his face, held just a trace of laughter. 'It is a nice thick slice you have there. Enough for both of us – do you not think?'

Thomas wasn't so sure. His hunger felt sharp as a rat's tooth in his belly. This one slice of bread was all that he was likely to get until lunch-time and his heart sank at the thought of having to give some of it away. But the old Grandmother had asked him.

And it was unthinkable that he should refuse.

Thomas was not one of the new breed of township children who scorn the old traditions and treat their elders with contempt. His grandmother had taught him to respect Age; if the Old One required him to share his breakfast with her, then share it he must. So he swallowed his reluctance, squatted down, and carefully broke the single slice of bread into two bits.

They came out not quite even, one half noticeably bigger than the other. Thomas weighed them in his hands, hesitating. Then, feeling the old woman's eyes on him, he quickly thrust the bigger portion into her hand and stuffed his own share into his mouth – all at once, half afraid that if he delayed, she might decide to ask for that as well.

For some moments they chewed together in silence. And the only sound was the busy smacking of lips. At length, the old woman brushed the crumbs from her lap and grunted, 'That was good. I thank you my son.' She sighed. 'But now I am thirsty. And my bottles are empty.'

She indicated two big plastic coke

containers that were lying in the weeds near her feet.

'That is all right Grandmother,' said Thomas obligingly. 'I will fetch you some water. I know where there's a tap.'

And he hopped to his feet, took up the two bottles and went trotting off with them under his arm.

It wasn't long before he was back again, his dark face shining with a sheen of sweat. He handed the gurgling bottles to the old woman and dropped thankfully into the shade beside her.

She drank greedily, and it was clear to see her thirst was very great. The first bottle was half empty when at last she wiped her hand across her mouth and set it down. Thomas took them both and dug them into the sandy soil, so they would not fall over. Then he sat quietly and watched her as she unhurriedly smoked her pipe; it would not be polite of him, as the younger person, to begin the conversation first.

After a time, she took the pipe out of her mouth, and her dark eyes, slow as the smoke, drifted over to him.

'What is your name, Small One?' she asked him. And when he told her, she said,

'I have not seen you here before. Where do you come from?'

Thomas explained that he lived in Wozani, that he had only come to Silverton for a small time to stay with his mother during the holidays. As soon as he mentioned his mother, the old woman wanted to know who she was. And which house she worked at, and whether it was a good job or a bad job. After that, he had to tell her about his house in Wozani – how many rooms it had, how many people lived in it; who the neighbours were, if they had work and whether they drank and so on and so forth. Following which, she wanted to know all about his grandmother too.

In no time, the Old One knew almost as much about Thomas's family and his family's business as he did himself. But he didn't mind her questions. He was used to the inquisitiveness of old ones; he knew how they liked to gossip – his grandmother was just the same. And besides, it was nice to have somebody taking an interest in him again.

Cross-legged in the weeds, he poured out to her all about his life in Wozani; his four sisters, especially his favourite one, Thandi.

He told her about his special friend Wiseman, the naughty boy, who had once captured his neighbour's chicken and plucked out all its feathers to make himself a head-dress for a game, leaving the poor bird to run around squawking, in just its skin, like a wrinkled lizard.

The Old One laughed a lot over that. But she stopped laughing when he went on to tell her about the troubles in the township.

He tried to explain to her about the Comrades and their struggle for freedom. But she snorted.

'They are fools, these Comrades. Do they think freedom can be won by burning and killing? It is delicate, it is like a bird; it must be captured gently, or it dies in your hands.'

She listened with grave attention as he related to her some of the events of the past months; the fighting between rival groups that made everyone so afraid; the houses that were burned, the people who disappeared – and no one knew whether they had been killed or taken by the police or gone into hiding.

He told her about the boy in his street who had been almost killed by a mob of youths because he had refused to join in the stoning of an enemy's house. And the time when some policemen had come bursting into Thomas's classroom in the middle of a lesson and dragged two of the older boys from their desks – with no explanation. When Thomas's teacher tried to stop them, they had hit him – in front of all the children. No one knew why the two boys had been taken away like that. But the next day, half the children were too scared to come to school – in case the police came for them next.

The old woman grew graver and graver, the longer that he spoke. Her pipe lay forgotten in her hands, and her fine eyes brimmed with sorrow.

'This land,' she said heavily, after long silence, 'has become a land of tears. I hear the weeping . . .' Her eyes, half-closed, stared unseeingly into the distance. 'It cries for the children. What will become of such children, who know only to speak the words of war? Who learn nothing but hatred and cruelty? Who have no childhood in their hearts? But how can it be otherwise?' she muttered on to herself. 'Everything is changing the old ways are gone. The children no longer are taught the ways of obedience. The elders have lost their authority; there is no more respect . . .'

She sighed and shook her head. Then took up her pipe again and absently knocked it clean. Her eyes fell on Thomas, and she smiled a little to see his solemn face.

'But you, Small One, you at least have respect,' she said. 'Your grandmother has taught you well.'

It was growing hotter. The shade of the fence was shrinking, drying up like water as the sun climbed higher. From the next street, came the sound of bicycles, and children's voices, shouting shrilly to each other. Thomas pictured the bright machines, circling and wheeling like restless horses. He took up his own home-made bicycle and began idly spinning its wire wheels.

'What is that you have there?' enquired the Old One curiously, holding out her hand. Shyly Thomas handed over the toy for her to see.

He had reason to be proud of his wire bicycle. He had spent many careful hours working on it, collecting the right bits of wire together, bending and fastening them into the exact shapes he required. And then fitting the parts together just right, so that the wheels turned and the pedals went round and the handlebars moved to left and right on the long steering column. His bicycle had real rubber for its tyres – cut from a discarded fanbelt. It had proper leather for its saddle, and rear reflectors cut out of cardboard and covered with coloured sweet-paper. It even boasted a tiny silver bell. No detail had been forgotten: he had wanted to make the bicycle as close to the real thing as he possibly could.

The old woman seemed greatly impressed by what she saw. 'This is very good,' she proclaimed at last. 'Did you make it yourself? You have clever hands and much patience,' she smiled. 'And you like bicycles, that I can see.'

'Oh yes,' Thomas told her eagerly, he did indeed like bicycles – very much! Did he have a bicycle of his own in Wozani, she wanted to know? No, unhappily he did not. There was nothing in the world that he would like better than a bicycle of his own. But . . . it was a problem. In his family, there was no money for bicycles. So he had to wait until he was grown.

Then, he would get a good job, that paid good money, and save until he had enough to buy his own bicycle.

The Old One took her pipe out of her mouth and laughed a soundless laugh. Her black eyes danced at him like a young girl's, and she said;

'That is a very long time for a boy to have to wait for something he wants – until he is not a boy any longer!'

She regarded him in silence for some seconds, her head cocked to one side like a curious bird.

'I will tell you what; I like you. You have given me your bread today and your company – and that is a precious gift for a young boy to give to an old woman like me. So I will make you a present in return – I will give you a bicycle.'

THE COMING OF QHIMLILI

Thomas stared at the Old One in astonishment, saying not a word. He could see she was waiting for him to say something but he was too confused to speak.

Where would an old woman like her, he was thinking to himself, who didn't even have money enough to buy her own breakfast, get a bicycle to give him? But to say so would be to insult her, and he had no wish to do that.

So he merely murmured, 'Thank you, Grandmother,' and quickly ducked his head, hoping she couldn't read his thoughts. But it seemed she could. For she gave a sudden grunt of laughter and said:

'What is the matter, Polite One, you do

not believe me? You are saying to yourself perhaps: "Where will a poor old woman like her get a bicycle from?" Is that not right?'

Thomas stirred uneasily, looking so guilty that she grunted again. 'Well, you are partly right. Old and poor I am. But I am more besides. I have knowledge of things that few in this world understand. Once, I was a person of Power! The Spirits talked to me. They liked me well, and favoured what I asked.' She sighed suddenly. 'But now, it is true, I am old. My strength is but a shadow of itself; I will need help to make the Spirits hear me.'

She shook her head and sighed again, frowning into the sunlight.

'I will call Qhimlili, who is far more ancient even than myself, but a Messenger of Power. You must sit still, Small One, and make no sound. Or he will not come.'

Then she rested her thin shoulders back against the fence-post, and let her eyelids fall. Thomas waited expectantly, holding his breath, not quite sure what was supposed to happen next.

Slow minutes passed. Among the sun-blasted weeds and grasses, only the insects moved. There was no sound save for the heavy droning of bees and flies.

The old woman sat very still, her face carved like a brown statue. Her breathing was deep and slow, and her eyelids flickered like nervous candles.

A finger of sunlight strayed onto her cheek and wandered slowly downwards. And for the first time, Thomas noticed the strange, shadowy scar that was stamped into the hollow place beneath the bone. It didn't resemble the usual tribal cuts that black women wore on their faces. This was more like a birthmark, or a brand, deeply etched into the cheek-bone flesh. And it had the form of a large, thin-limbed tree.

Thomas's eyes studied the scar with interest, noting the clear outline of stem and branches, the pattern of upswept limbs and dotted crown of leaves. Curiously, he leaned forward so that he could examine it more closely. But as he did, the Old One's voice came hissing at him, freezing him in his place. 'Be still! The Messenger has come.'

Her eyes opened suddenly. And there was such a strangeness in them, that Thomas was afraid.

They were staring not at him, but past him, at a point just beyond his left shoulder.

He tried to follow their focus without moving his head, rolling his eyes sideways as far as they would go and cricking his chin around inch by inch, until he had a view of what was behind him.

And there, on the pile of broken bricks nearby, he spied a large, blue-headed lizard, of the kind that is called Qhimlili. It was standing so still that he almost didn't see it at all. Its crusty grey-brown body blended perfectly with the bricks' dusty colours. Its wrinkled throat was stretched tautly upwards, as though in worship. And its round, black eyes stared straight at the old woman's face.

'Qhimlili,' she crooned to it, swaying her body back and forth, 'Qhimlili, who is agile like the wind. Qhimlili, who knows the secrets of rock and tree. Qhimlili, the Ancient One, whom the Spirits love.'

Her voice rose and fell like strange music. The lizard seemed to be listening to what she said. It strained towards her more intently than ever, its blue head arched back in concentration, its wide mouth agape.

Thomas felt the goose-bumps rise on his flesh. He dared not move or breathe or even blink. Something was happening between the lizard and the old woman that he didn't understand. A sorcery had crept into the hot, drowsy air of the lot; he felt that anything might happen then – anything at all.

He couldn't have said whether one minute or ten went by in this fashion, but there came a moment when he realised with a start that the lizard was gone. He hadn't seen it disappear; it simply wasn't there any longer.

Beside him, the Old One was stirring, stretching herself and yawning as though wakening from sleep. She looked at him with eyes that seemed to see him again. Her voice, when she spoke, sounded tired and spent.

'It is done; you will have your bicycle. Not far from here, you will find it waiting for you – under the Spirit Tree that grows on the hillside above the river. Do you know that place?'

'No,' stammered Thomas, he did not know it.

'Well, it is not hard to reach. I will tell you the way. But you must not go there until the sun is setting. If you go before, you will find nothing. Do you understand?'

Thomas nodded; and she proceeded to give him directions, making him say them back to her three times until she was satisfied that he knew them by heart.

'Good,' she nodded at last. 'But remember – wait until the sun is gone before you go there. Now I must rest. This has taken all my power; I am empty of strength.'

She prised herself stiffly off the ground and adjusted her blanket around her. Thomas helped her collect her pipe and water bottles from the ground. He thanked her earnestly for all her trouble – trying to sound as if he really believed what she had said that he really would find a bicycle waiting there for him on some hillside underneath a tree! But as he watched her shuffle off into the shadows of the bushes, his thoughts were full of doubt.

She was old, this Gogo, he reminded himself. She had all her teeth still, but after all, she was very old, and age brought foolishness. It was tempting to believe her talk and promises, very tempting. But it was unlikely that they were true. For after all, it was not possible, one did not simply conjure up bicycles out of the empty air.

Then he remembered the lizard – Qhimlili the Messenger had he not seen him with his own eyes? Yes – but what exactly *was* it he had seen? Nothing but an ordinary lizard, perched on a pile of bricks, enjoying the sunshine. It was only the old woman's talk that had made him believe there was strangeness in it.

Thus did Thomas argue with himself all the way home. Once there however, he soon succeeded in putting the old woman and her far-fetched promise from his mind. For this day was Thursday, his mother's half-day off. And the afternoon was filled with pleasant distractions.

First, there was lunch – a steaming plateful of corn porridge and curried beans and bread to take the bite out of his hunger. And afterwards, an expedition to the big shopping centre on the main road at the bottom of the hill. This took some time to reach, not just because the hill was long and the day exceedingly hot, but because his mother had to keep stopping to greet and gossip with friends along the way.

They reached the stores at last, and while his mother did her shopping and found more friends to gossip with, Thomas wandered around, contentedly sucking on an ice-cream, looking in the windows with their bright Christmas displays and watching the security guards search the bags and packages of all the customers, to make sure they weren't carrying any weapons.

His mother took a long time with her shopping, for the stores were crowded and the queues long. But at last she was finished. Then came the long, long haul back up the steep hill again, this time laden with heavy packages: corn meal and eggs and flour; sugar, sour milk and big litre bottles of Coke. For his mother would be having friends round to visit at her kia that evening, and must have food to offer them.

As soon as they got back, she went inside to start her preparations. Thomas was kept busy for a time with various errands – sweeping out the kia, scrubbing the cooking pots clean, fetching and carrying. But at last there was nothing more for him to do.

Thankfully he escaped out of the hot, stuffy room and wandered into the cooler air outside. Only then, left to himself again, did his thoughts turn back to the old woman and the promised bicycle.

JOURNEY
AT SUNSET

It was almost evening. The sun was low on the horizon, the gardens soft with creeping shadow. Thomas hung over the railings at the top of the house and watched the evening clouds massing thickly above the tree-tops. He heard the Old One's voice in his mind, as clearly as if she were speaking into his ear, reciting her careful instructions for him to memorize.

He whispered them to himself. And his heart began to thud like a busy drum inside his chest. Really, he thought, it might be fun to follow her directions after all; to go to that place she had mentioned – even if he found no bicycle there, and just have a look. Because really, he had nothing better to do at this moment anyway.

So he let his bare feet take him down the driveway, along the street and into the next one; past the shadowy lot, with its half-glimpsed figures moving in the gloom beyond the broken fence. The roads were busy at this hour, crowded with home-coming traffic. Car doors slammed in the driveways. Children and dogs rushed out to greet returning masters. No one spared Thomas a glance. The people of the area were used to him now – the small black boy, who wandered through their white neighbourhood like a visitor from another planet.

Thomas trotted along quickly, at home in these streets, picking out the old woman's landmarks without difficulty; down the wide, straight road that led past the school playing fields; past the bright pink house that perched like a strange, iced cake in its green box of garden; round this corner and that corner, and up the twisting zigzag of a hill. There, at the top, he found the flight of rough stone steps that cut down through the steep hillside, providing a convenient short-cut to the valley below.

Swiftly Thomas galloped down them, his bare feet slapping against the stone, his stomach shivery with excitement. The sun had slipped away, leaving a sky full of changing colour. Hadeda birds were hurrying by with their harsh, anxious cries, warning that darkness was not far off.

Before him was unfamiliar territory – a nest of quiet roads and big, important-looking houses, set in a seclusion of natural bush. Somewhere in their midst, he must find the grassy track that would lead him to the river – and whatever lay beyond.

He walked uncertainly along the shadowed pavements. These streets were much more private than the ones above. There were few passers-by here, and strangers were clearly not welcomed. With every step he took, Thomas felt more and more uncomfortable. The people from the houses looked at him suspiciously, as though they thought he had come to rob them. Dogs barked madly from all directions, each one sparking off the frenzy of its neighbours, until it seemed as if the whole neighbourhood was in uproar with the hysterical racket.

By the time Thomas found the dead-end street he had been searching for, he was in a sweat of nerves. He crept timidly down the length of the cul-de-sac, wishing he could make himself invisible – all too aware of the unfriendly eyes that watched his progress from the verandas and lawns. This way and that way he peered as he walked, trying to spot the river-track; staring between houses, up driveways, into gardens – terrified that he might miss it and have to retrace his steps all the way back again, past the same barking dogs and stony faces.

He was nearing the end of the cul-de-sac, with no success, and was just passing by a big house that bristled with burglar bars and security gates and notices warning trespassers to 'Beware!' when he heard a loud voice bellowing at him:

'Hey you! Boy!'

A big, burly white man came striding down the driveway towards him, two enormous black dogs leaping and barking at his side.

'What do you think you're doing, hey?'

'Nothing, Master,' stammered Thomas, trying not to move a muscle as the dogs bounded forward growling to sniff over him.

'Don't talk rubbish to me,' said the man. 'You must be doing something here. I want to know what.'

'No, Master, I'm not doing nothing Master. Only looking for . . . for . . .' But Thomas's English had deserted him. Not for the life of him could he think of the words he needed.

'Ya, I know what you're looking for – something to steal!' The man's face was red with anger and suspicion. 'You think I don't know what you're up to, hey? Bladdy little rubbish! I've been watching you – looking into all the houses to see what you can swipe. I should set my dogs on you!'

'No, Master!' Thomas felt hot and cold all over. 'I'm not trying to steal nothing Master! Just looking . . . for the water . . . for the way to the river. If Master can just show me the path, I will go there now.'

'You bladdy well better,' growled the man. He jerked his thumb over his shoulder. 'It's over there. Now voetsak! And don't let me catch you here again, or I'll tell my dogs to catch you.'

'Yes, Master – no, Master – thank you Master!'

Backing away from the dogs, Thomas hurried over to where the man had pointed.

The track was there all right. He had

already walked past it once, mistaking it for part of somebody's lawn. It ran between two unwalled gardens, curving round the backs of the houses and then dipping out of sight.

Breathing heavily, Thomas ran along its grassy softness, still shaking inside from his encounter with the red-faced man. How thankful he was to leave that unfriendly street behind him at last!

The track was becoming narrower and narrower, bumping swiftly downwards, leaving the houses behind. Soon, he was in a different world.

On either side of him rose walls of reedy vegetation, thickly choked with thorny growth and weeds and tough, matted trees. They closed out the light and swallowed up the air, making the atmosphere as dim and steamy as a jungle. There was no sound of birds or insects here, no rustling of wind-stirred leaves just a close, pressing silence.

Thomas wasn't altogether sure he liked this place. It was gloomy, secretive, unfriendly. There could be anything hiding in these reedy thickets – snakes, *tsotsis*, evil spirits – anything!

He turned to look behind him through

the false twilight of branches, wondering
whether he should turn back while he still
could. But then he thought of the red-faced
man, with his threatening words and his big
dogs, besides, he would never forgive
himself if he turned back now, when he was
so close to his journey's end.

The track had become very steep. The
grass had disappeared, and Thomas's toes
sank into a slippery ooze – unpleasant-
smelling and alive with hungry mosquitos.
They swarmed excitedly about his bare legs
and feet, dug their needle-mouths into a
hundred places on his skin, driving him mad
with itching.

But he dared not stop to scratch. If he
stopped, something might jump at him from
the bushes. Or a bad spirit might settle on
his shoulder – he was sure there were bad
spirits here! Why had the old woman sent
him to this place? Even the birds knew
better than to come here. There was
something in the air that wasn't right.

The smell was growing worse. He looked
down and saw ahead of him a greenish
trickle, oozing sluggishly across his track. It
took several moments before he realised that
this was the 'river' that the old woman had

referred to. Now he knew where the awful smell was coming from. And why.

High above him, at the top of a steep, muddy bank that bordered the stinking water, was a big, concrete waste pipe. And it was from this that the contamination came – smelly streams of it that dribbled in channels down the hillside and emptied themselves into the dead river bed.

Thomas shook his head. He thought it a very careless thing for people to kill a river in this manner. Evidently, they were people who did not understand the preciousness of water. Water, in the white city, was very plentiful. It came gushing easily out of every tap. Rivers did not have the same importance here as they did for those who lived where there were no taps.

Still shaking his head, he cleared the shameful trickle with one leap and began to scramble up the slippery bank towards the pipeline.

Soon, to his relief, he was standing at the top of the hillside above the gloom and closeness of the river-bush, drawing in deep lungfuls of untainted air. Out here in the open, the twilight lay more softly. Birds flew back and forth on their way home to roost, and in the valley below, the houses were just beginning to show their lights.

Thomas began to feel more cheerful again. He followed the line of the pipe away from the river-bank, hurrying again, not from fear this time, but anticipation. And then he came around the further curve of the hillside and he stopped dead, his breath catching in his throat, he had come to the end of his journey.

THE
SPIRIT TREE

Before him was a tree – a large tree, that loomed ghost-pale against the deepening sky. It leaned out over the slope of the hillside like a man surveying his land. Its limbs were long and tangled, twisting up in skeletal fingers from the pale trunk. Its grey leaves twitched and trembled as they brushed the sky.

It wasn't a type of tree that Thomas was familiar with, but he recognised it at once. He had seen its image earlier that day, stamped into the living flesh of the old woman's cheek. Wonder and apprehension shivered through him, did this mean that she was indeed what she had claimed to be? Could it be possible that she had spoken the truth to him after all?

With tiptoeing steps, he moved over the hillside, so full of suspense that he could hardly breathe. The Spirit Tree seemed to watch him with invisible eyes. He could hear its leaves and branches whispering as they rubbed against each other, and the sound was full of secrecy. Eagerly as Thomas walked, he scanned the ground around the trunk, fully expecting to see a bicycle take shape there in the dusky gloom. But no, there was no bicycle.

He made two circles around the tree, just to be sure. He even stood underneath and stared up into the branches in case it had been wedged into a fork. But no, there definitely was no bicycle.

Shrugging, he tried to swallow his disappointment. Had he not suspected all along that it would be this way, that the old woman's talk was nothing but the foolishness of age? Why then should he feel such disappointment now?

A movement, stealthy and slight, caught his eye. He turned his head sharply and saw, on the pale, pale trunk of the tree, some darker shadow. The shadow moved, became a tailed, crusty-bodied thing that plopped to the ground and scuttled off into the grass.

Thomas caught a quick glimpse of a wrinkled blue head.

'Qhimlili!' he breathed, his voice squeaking in his throat. Qhimlili the Lizard – here, at the Spirit Tree? But surely this was more than chance! Surely this was the very same Qhimlili that the old woman had summoned to the lot that morning, Qhimlili the Spirit Messenger.

Cold worms of excitement wriggled up and down between his shoulder-blades. He fixed his eyes on the trunk of the tree, and his heart almost stopped beating. For there, right where the lizard had lain, was a shadow he hadn't noticed before. It was a long and narrow crack and it ran, like a secret compartment, all the way down the smooth surface of the trunk.

It smiled at him with rough, dark lips. It invited him to put his fingers in, and feel inside. For a long time, Thomas stood there, mistrustfully staring at it. At last, very cautiously, mindful of the lizard and other things that liked to lurk in holes, he reached his hand inside.

THE SECRET
IN THE TREE

His fingers brushed something. Something that wasn't tree. Thomas jerked his hand back so sharply that he knocked himself on the chin. He looked at his fingers with round, white eyes, then back at the tree again. What had he touched? It had been cold, as a snake is cold. But it hadn't moved. And nothing came leaping at him from the narrow blackness.

He waited a few moments more to be sure, then bent his knees and brought his face close to the wood, shutting first one eye, then the other, squinting into the crack. But he couldn't see anything, neither shape nor movement. He turned his head and pressed his ear where his eye had been, but there was no sound either. Whatever it was in there, it was keeping very quiet. Perhaps it was alive and perhaps not. There was only one way to find out.

Thomas closed his eyes and plunged his hand back into the crack.

Again his fingers touched it; a cold, hard, puzzling thing. This time, he didn't withdraw his hand, but closed his grip around the coldness and held on tight, at the same time tugging hard. There was a sucking sound, like a cork popping out of a bottle. And the next moment, something came rolling backwards out of the crack with such momentum that Thomas was knocked flat. He felt a heaviness crash down on top of him, pinning his legs; he glimpsed pedals and handlebars, spinning wheels.

'Hau!' he whispered, his eyes almost popping out of his head, staring and staring at the impossible sight. And then again, 'Hau!'

It was all he could say. Above his head, the Spirit Tree shook and quivered with secret laughter. He lifted his dazed eyes to stare at it, wondering if perhaps it had bewitched him – worked some kind of magic on his eyes so that they only *thought* they saw a bicycle where in fact there was none.

But the pain of metal angles digging into his flesh was real enough.

Thomas gathered his wits with an effort and slid himself out from under the tangle of pedals and wheels, lifting the bicycle carefully to stand beside him, where he could examine it better. And as he saw its beauty, his knees went weak.

For what a bicycle this was! Fit for the son of a chief to ride!

It looked brand new. Even in the fading light of dusk, he could see how its newness shone. It had been painted two different colours, one half as red as flame, the other, dazzling blue. Gold specks glittered in the paintwork. Its handlebars curved like graceful butterflies. Its saddle was as soft to the touch as a horse's nose.

'Magical!' Thomas breathed over and over again, running his palms over the sleek lines and textures, gazing and gazing as if he would never get his fill.

He felt as if his heart would burst with longing. He felt he would give anything to own this wonderful bicycle – anything in the world, if only it could be his.

But of course he couldn't keep it. A

bicycle such as this one didn't come from nowhere. Not even a Spirit Messenger could conjure such finery from empty air.

No, this bicycle belonged to somebody. Clearly, it had been stolen, and the thief had hidden it in the crack in the Spirit Tree. Was it the old woman who had stolen it? But she was too old, she would never have managed to bring it here, all the way up that steep bank by herself. Yet she must know something about it; had she not told him he would find it here, in this exact spot?

For long moments Thomas stood, lost in thought. What he should do, he at last decided, was go back home; tell his mother the whole story and ask her advice. She would know better than he did, what must be done. But first, he must put the bicycle back in its hiding place.

He grasped its handlebars, rolled it up to the tree and tried to push it, front wheel first, back into the crack – the way he had found it. But of course it wouldn't go. Its handlebars were much too broad to fit through the crack's narrow mouth.

So then he turned it around and tried to push it in backwards. The rear wheel rolled in without trouble. But then the pedals caught. And no amount of pushing or shoving would force them through.

Thomas wrestled with the stubborn thing for quite a time. At last he gave up – cross, panting and not a little mystified.

Was this not the very same crack, he asked himself, from which he had tugged the bicycle just a short while before? Yes, undoubtedly it was. Then why could he not now fit the bicycle back inside again? But to that he had no answer.

He sat down to think, resting the bicycle across his lap, unable to bring himself to put it down. The moon was rising, glowing in the sky, scattering its pale light over the hillside. Bats were flitting to and fro like tiny phantoms. Somewhere close by, a bullfrog burst into loud croaking. Overhead, the Spirit Tree whispered and shook. Yet Thomas wasn't afraid. He felt that the bicycle protected him. The weight of it across his lap was a comfort and a shield.

He knew it must be very late. There would be trouble waiting for him when he reached home. But he didn't care. All he wanted was to sit there for a while longer with this beautiful bicycle, and pretend that it was his.

He stroked his fingers lovingly across its painted smoothness. There was some writing on the frame below the saddle that he hadn't noticed before. The moonlight seemed to bring it to life – shiny gold lettering that looped boldly from one side of the cross-bar to the other. He craned his head sideways, struggling to read it upside down.

Slowly he spelt the letters out;

'I – n – y – o – s – i.'

Thomas's heart tumbled over. *Inyosi!* But that was his name – his own special name, that his grandmother had given him because he loved sweet things so much. It meant 'the honey-bee'. Not even his friends called him Inyosi; yet here it was, written in flashing gold along the crossbar of this bicycle.

Then Thomas believed at last that this bicycle belonged to no one else, but to *him*. The old woman had procured it for him, exactly as she had promised. For her promise had not been empty talk at all, but the word of a Sorceress!

And at that thought, Thomas trembled. Cold sweat broke out on his forehead as he considered how differently his encounter with her might have ended.

What, for instance, if he had refused her his bread this morning? Or displeased her in some other accidental way? Then perhaps she would have used her sorcery on him quite differently – not for his happiness, but for his ruin.

Sobered by the thought, he clambered to his feet. But he couldn't stay serious for long. His heart was singing, lifting in his chest like a joyous bird. He took up his bicycle, curling his fingers tightly around its coloured grips, and wheeled it proudly along the moonlit hillside.

It came with him smoothly, easily, like a docile horse. He manoeuvred it down the steep bank above the river with no trouble at all. And when they had crossed the stinking water, and started into the thick and airless darkness along the path, he hardly felt nervous at all.

For the bicycle lit his way. The thin yellow beam from its small headlight went before him, stabbing a path through the blackness. He knew that no bad spirits would dare to interfere with him now; not when he had his magical bicycle to protect him!

MAGICAL BICYCLE

Thomas hardly slept that night. Partly, it was because his bottom was still smarting from the hiding he had received. His mother had been very angry when he finally crept into the crowded kia, smelling like dead fish, she said, and covered in mud as if he had been swimming in it. It was only because such behaviour was unusual for him that he escaped further punishment. But Thomas wouldn't have cared that night if she had smacked him with ten slippers.

Nothing could spoil the mood of happiness that was upon him. As he lay awake in the hot, dark room, with its lingering smells of cooking and bodies, all he could think about was his bicycle – safely stowed away in its hiding place at

59

the back of the kia. He kept wanting to jump up and run outside to check that it was still there. His hands itched to curve themselves again around the slender handlebars; he could hardly wait for dawn to come so that he could go down into the street and attempt his first ride.

Walking home from the river that evening, Thomas had had plenty of time to think. And what he had chiefly thought, was that he was going to have a very difficult time of it trying to explain to people where he had acquired his new bicycle.

No one who set eyes on it was going to believe it wasn't stolen. It was too new, too smart, too expensive-looking. Where would a poor black boy like him get such a thing? they would ask themselves. Soon, the police would be asking that question too. And when he told them his story about the old sorceress in the lot, about Qhimlili the Messenger, and the crack in the Spirit Tree, they would not believe it. Even if they went to the lot themselves and questioned the Old One, they would not believe it. They would say, as he had said, that she was old and full of foolishness. Or perhaps they would say that she was lying too, that she had helped

Thomas to steal his bicycle.

Either way, they would take the bicycle away from him. They would throw him and the Old One into the police van together, and drive them both off to jail.

All this Thomas had been able to imagine with painful clearness on the endless journey back home from the river. It was then that he had come to his decision. The only way he could be sure of keeping his bicycle, was if no one knew he had it. Therefore, he must share his secret with no one – not even his mother. He must keep his bicycle hidden away behind the kia. And only in the very early morning, when it was unlikely that there would be other people about, would he allow himself to take it into the street, and ride it.

Lying there wakeful on his narrow mattress, it seemed to Thomas as if the morning would never come. He tossed and he turned, listening enviously to his mother's peaceful breathing. Every time he did manage to doze off, he would wake again with a start, certain that the dawn must have arrived, only to find the sky beyond the kia window as dark as ever.

Finally, he gave up trying to sleep at all.

He rose very quietly, and let himself out into the night.

The moon had set. Big white cloud masses drifted soundlessly between the stars. Only the croaking of the bull-frogs disturbed the peace of the sleeping world. Thomas crept round on soft feet to the back of the kia. He hardly dared to look, so afraid was he that he might find his bicycle had vanished. But it was there, waiting for him, glimmering faintly in the starlight, as if in welcome – his magical bicycle.

Gently he eased it from its hiding place and bumped it down the steps, to the bottom of the driveway.

The street was quiet as sleep itself. Not a person was in sight, not a car, not even a dog to spoil the solitude. The street-lamps seemed to watch him with their harsh, electric eyes. For a second, he felt a jolt of nervousness run through him. But the bicycle was beside him, as always, giving him courage. Taking a deep breath, he lifted his leg and swung himself onto the saddle.

It welcomed his bottom like a soft, leather hand. The rubber grips on the handlebars felt snug and cool beneath his sweating palms. For a while, he simply sat there, his dark eyes shining with delight.

'I *like* you, Bicycle,' he murmured breathlessly, leaning down to rub his cheek against the handlebars. 'You're . . . you're *magical!*'

He felt a movement underneath his cheekbone. The handlebars swung suddenly out of his hands, and the front wheel, like a turning head, drifted slowly round, as though to look at him. Smiling, he sat up and drew the handlebars back towards him.

But a second time they nudged themselves free of his fingers. And there was the front wheel again, looking at him. The glinting of its metal spokes in the lamplight looked so much like grinning teeth, that Thomas was unnerved.

'Haai Wena!' he muttered, jerking the handlebars straight, ready to leap off and run if the bicycle showed any further signs of uncanny life. But to his relief, it was quiet now, standing meekly underneath him, as a bicycle should.

'Okey-dokey,' he said softly, copying Kevin. He drew his breath slowly in, then let it out again. 'Okey-dokey.'

He lifted one foot to the pedals, and with the other, propelled himself a short way along the street, listening with pleasure to the lovely click-clicking sounds that the wheels made. The bicycle seemed pleased to have him aboard. It positively purred as he trundled it along. Every now and then, the front wheel would swing inwards, and he would catch a flash of those thin teeth, grinning at him. But now he just grinned back, too full of excitement to feel perturbed.

Half-way down the street, he stopped and turned the bicycle around. Carefully he prepared for his big moment, fussing about in the saddle, winding the pedals around until they were in just the right position for his feet. Then he took a deep breath, gripped his toes around the hard edge of rubber and, very daring, lifted his second foot from the floor.

Many, many bruises later, it was a very glum and weary Thomas who propped his bicycle against a lamppost and limped over to the grass verge for a rest.

He had not guessed that bicycle-riding involved such difficulty. The bicycle children made it look so easy; they simply hopped on, and off they sailed. He felt he would give anything to be able to do the same.

His problem was, he just couldn't get going. He never seemed able to keep his seat long enough to get the bicycle in motion. As soon as he lifted his feet to the pedals, while he was still struggling to push them round, his balance would fail him and over he would go, toppling sideways like a sack of stones.

The bicycle tried to help him. He would feel it, swaying wildly underneath him, straining to hold itself upright under his unsteady weight. But each time, it would lose the battle and there they would be on the tarmac again – usually with him underneath the bicycle, cushioning its fall. And he would have yet more bruises and scraped places to add to his collection.

Sighing, Thomas rested his chin in his hands, and stared despondently into the shadowed street. He was growing very tired of all these falls, he told the listening street-lights. There must be an easier way to learn to ride than this! If only he had someone here to help him, to hold him up until he had the pedals working. Or better still, if he could find some way to get the bicycle moving *without* pedalling at all . . .

Slowly he took his hands from his chin, and turned his head. He stared along the street, to the part where it began to rise, gathering itself gently into a small, swelling hump before levelling off again to meet the corner. It was that spot, Thomas remembered, that Kevin usually made for when he wanted to try out one of his famous stunts. It was much easier to get going from a slope than a straight, he had once heard him say.

Thomas smiled grimly to himself. He fetched the bicycle, and marched it over to the little rise, wheeling it up to the very highest point. Then he swung himself onto the saddle and sat there, breathing quickly, trying to work up the nerve to start down.

It wasn't a very steep slope, for someone who could ride. But to Thomas, it seemed to plunge like a cliff. If he fell off while he was speeding down – as he very likely would – he would hurt himself and, what was worse, he might damage the bicycle.

But he was allowed no time to dwell on such thoughts. The bicycle gave a sudden lurch beneath him. And before he knew what was happening, they were rolling forward, plunging down the gradient, faster and faster, leaving his stomach behind them.

Thomas clung to the handlebars for all he was worth, his teeth locked together, not daring to move a muscle in case he fell off. He forgot he had brakes. He forgot he could slow down the motion of the bicycle whenever he wanted to. All he knew was that the street was rushing by him in a dark torrent. There was air flying into his face, a sensation more wonderful than anything he had felt before.

And then it was over. Too soon, the street was levelling off again. The bicycle was slowing, faltering, losing its momentum. Quickly Thomas drove down on the pedals, pumping them round and round with unsteady legs. The bicycle swayed like a drunken ship. The front wheel wobbled wildly, and for an awful moment, he was certain they must fall again. But this time, they didn't fall. They swerved on to the end of the street, unsteady, but still upright. And . . . he was riding! Thomas wanted to cheer, to shout, to call everyone to come and look at him. He was riding! He felt like the King of the World.

Dawn came at last, breaking over the eastern roof-tops, reaching its soft, pink fingers into the gardens and streets. The birds woke up and began to call and twitter. In some of the houses, lights went on; Thomas didn't notice.

Again and again he took his bicycle back to the top of the small rise and sent himself speeding downhill. By degrees, his skill and confidence increased until there came a point when he no longer needed the slope to get himself started at all.

Up the street and down the street he sailed, lost in his private dream, aware of nothing but his bicycle. The pedals sang a soft song as he drove them round and round. The tyres whispered against the road. The little silver bell jingled sweet tunes to itself.

It was the sound of a car starting up in the next yard that brought him back to earth again at last. He looked up and saw with a start how light the world had grown. There was movement in the houses, a sound of dishes clattering from kitchen windows. It was time to take his bicycle inside.

He could hardly make it up the driveway, for his legs trembled like jelly from the unaccustomed exercise and he ached in every muscle from his many falls. But he forced himself to hurry, spurred on by the fear that someone from the Madam's house might look outside and see him before he could get his bicycle upstairs.

He was only just in time. As he came round to the front of the kia after leaving the bicycle in its hiding place, the door opened and his mother stepped out, yawning and sleepy-eyed in her pink uniform. She wanted to know where he'd been.

He explained to her that he had found it too hot to sleep, and so had risen early to go outside. She seemed satisfied enough with the answer, but Thomas felt guilty for the rest of the day.

He didn't like lying to his mother. It made him feel very uncomfortable. Yet what else, he asked himself, could he have done? If he told her the truth, he knew what would happen; she would take one look at his bicycle, and insist that it must be stolen. She would make him take it down to the police station, and give it up to them. Thomas's heart went cold at the very thought.

No, better that he should lie, he thought defiantly, than have his bicycle taken away from him; this bicycle which was *his*, which even had his *name* on it. But he still felt guilty.

Every morning after that, it was the same. Thomas would wake in the darkness before dawn, some mysterious clock inside his body telling him, through his sleep, that it was time to rise.

Only half-awake, he would steal out of the kia, collect his bicycle, and wheel it down into the street. Then off they would go, sailing into the dark morning, into the sleeping kingdom of the city.

Each day, they became bolder, venturing further and further away from home, gradually leaving familiar streets behind them, eager to explore. The city was theirs – an eerie place in this quiet hour, where only the ghosts were awake. But Thomas felt no fear. His bicycle had a magic in it; it protected him, it would always protect him, from any danger.

With each day that went by, his love for it grew fiercer. It truly was a most wonderful machine, constantly surprising him. There was nothing, it seemed, that it couldn't do, nowhere it couldn't take him. It leapt easily up the steepest hills, across the most broken ground. Along the smoother stretches, it flew like a racehorse, soundless and swift.

Its spinning wheels would scarcely seem to touch the ground. Thomas would feel the wind of its speed vibrating through him, lifting him up as if he were flying. Then, in the dream of motion, he was no longer Thomas – he was *Umfana Womoya* – he was the boy of the wind. And in such moments, he would understand, truly, what Freedom was. It was this, this speeding through the lonely morning with his heart lifting up like a bird and the whole world his. No one to tell him he wasn't allowed to go here, that he mustn't do this, that he must get away to his own place.

And then he would wonder; was this what the Comrades were fighting for? Or when they talked of Freedom, did they mean something else? He would have liked to ask the Old One about it. He felt sure that she would know.

He had been back more than once to the lot to try and find her so he could say his thanks. He had even brought small gifts of fruit and bread that he had saved from his own meals to give her. But he never found her there. Perhaps she didn't want to be found. Or perhaps some misfortune had come to her. After all, she was old.

Whatever the reason, Thomas was sorry. She was the one person who shared the secret of his bicycle. With her, he could have spoken freely of its wonders. He was bursting to speak of it to someone. It made him sad not to be able to show it off, to have to keep it hidden away as if he were ashamed of it. Each day, he found it harder and harder to have to turn for home just when the world was waking up, when the sky was rosy with new light and his blood sang with the song of riding. He grew more and more careless about staying out later than he should.

Often, daybreak would find him very far from home. And he would have to race back through streets filling with early morning traffic, hoping against hope that he wouldn't be stopped, or that no one from his mother's neighbourhood would recognise him.

Usually, by the time he arrived back, his mother would already be at work in the kitchen. And he would have to creep around the side of the house like a criminal, his heart in his mouth in case she chanced to look up at the wrong moment and catch sight of him through the window.

She was used to his early morning risings now and no longer questioned him about them. But his deception continued to fill him with shame. He felt that he didn't deserve his happiness. It was not a good son, who lied to his mother and kept secrets hidden from her. In his heart, he felt that his good fortune could not last. Something must happen to take his undeserved happiness away from him. One day, it almost did.

ENCOUNTER WITH BAD BOYS

On a particular morning, Thomas was speeding home – late as usual – taking a short-cut through a quiet alleyway, when he almost rode full tilt into three black boys, who were turning into the narrow lane from the other side.

'Hey, Silly Goat! Watch what you're doing!' one of them called indignantly, skipping nimbly out of the way.

Thomas mumbled his apologies and dismounted to pull his bicycle to one side so they would have room to pass. He was hoping fervently that they would pass; one look at these boys was enough to warn him they were trouble.

They weren't much older than Thomas, and yet they seemed very old. Their faces were hard and their eyes were bold and their walk was full of swagger. They were dressed in ragged shirts and torn trousers. And they carried in their hands, empty bags which, no doubt, they were intending to fill with things that didn't belong to them.

These were some of the *izigebengu* – bad boys – that Thomas's mother and the Madam had been complaining about only the day before. They came into the white areas, supposedly to ask for jobs, but really, to steal whatever they could get their hands on. It didn't matter to them whether the people they stole from were black or white, rich or poor. They were a nuisance to all alike.

Now, seeing Thomas standing nervously before them with his beautiful brand-new bicycle, they began to grin and nudge each other. The biggest of the three handed his bags to the others and strolled forward with his hands in his pockets.

'Mmmmm, Little Goat,' he said, pretending to be admiring. 'That's some smart bike you've got there, isn't it?'

'Yes,' said Thomas miserably, tightening his hold on the handlebars, wondering whether he should try and make a run for it while he still could. He could guess well enough what was coming. He looked up and down the alleyway, hoping against hope that someone would appear to rescue him. But there was no one in sight. 'I must say, I like it,' continued the big boy, walking round the bike and making a great show of examining it from all angles. 'I wouldn't mind one like that for myself. What do you say, Brothers?'

'It sure is smart,' agreed the second boy. While the third just sniggered.

'It must have cost a lot,' the big boy continued thoughtfully.

'Where do you suppose a silly goat like him got the money to buy it?'

'Maybe he has a rich daddy!'

'Maybe he *didn't* buy it!'

'Maybe he *stole* it!' all three shouted in chorus.

'No!' said Thomas quickly. 'I didn't steal it. It's *my* bicycle!'

'Well then, you must be very rich. Rich like the white people.'

The big boy looked him up and down with his hard black eyes.

'Me and my friends we don't like rich boys. You see how poor we are.' He indicated his torn clothing. 'We have no money like you, to buy nice things like this smart bicycle. When we find something we like, we have to just take it.'

'But I am not rich,' said Thomas in a very small voice. 'I did not buy this bicycle. I . . . I just found it.'

The big boy guffawed. The one standing next to him grinned and blew his nose on his fingers, wiping them casually on his stained pants.

'He found it he says!' remarked the big boy mockingly, to no one in particular.

'But I did!' insisted Thomas hopelessly. 'I really did – I found it; it belonged to nobody.'

'Yes, yes,' said the big boy, 'we know all about it. We also "find" things – don't we, Brothers? Now this must be our lucky day. Because we've just "found" your bicycle!'

'You think you still remember how to ride, Chief?' asked the second boy mockingly. And the third said,

'Don't kill this bicycle the way you killed the other one!'

The big boy made a rude sign at them with his fingers. He sauntered towards Thomas, his hand confidently outstretched.

'Give me the bicycle.'

'No!' whimpered Thomas.

'Give it here, I said!'

'I won't – it's mine! It's a special bicycle –
it even has my name on it! I won't let you
take it!'

'Oh you won't?'

The big boy raised his hands and brought
them down in a vicious chop across
Thomas's wrists. Thomas cried out, and let
go of the bicycle, which fell with a clatter.
The big boy gave him a hard shove in the
chest, making him stagger back into the
arms of the boys behind. One of them
grabbed his shoulder and twisted his arm
painfully up behind his back, holding him so
that he couldn't move.

The big boy sauntered forward. He put
his face very close to Thomas's. His breath
smelled bad. His eyes were an unhealthy
yellow colour. They frightened Thomas;
there was no kindness in them.

'You see, Silly Goat. It is better to obey
when I speak politely. That way you don't
get hurt.'

Thomas said nothing. The pain of his
twisted arm was making it hard for him to
breathe. He was afraid that if he tried to

move or speak, it would be twisted even more.

The third boy meanwhile, had gone forward and picked up the fallen bicycle. He turned it round, threw a cheeky glance over his shoulder at the big boy, and hopped into the saddle.

They all watched as he wobbled off down the alley, perched like a grasshopper, his long, skinny thighs sticking out sideways, his bony back so thin you could count every knob.

'Smart hey, My Brother,' the big boy called. 'You like our new bike?'

The skinny one hunched his shoulders gleefully, and lifted a triumphant hand. A second later, that hand was all they could see of him; he had disappeared! One moment he was sitting on the bicycle, gaily waving to them, and the next, he had vanished somewhere over the handlebars.

The bicycle had simply seemed to buck him off. They saw it lift its rear end into the air like a pitching horse; and that was the end of its rider.

A few seconds later when the bicycle tumbled down beside him, he was sitting there, still in his riding position, as though astride an imaginary saddle, looking dazed and astonished.

'What happened?' he asked groaningly, as he raised himself off his bruised cheeks and limped back to the others.

His friends were laughing too hard to answer.

'You hit a stone or something,' gasped the big boy finally. 'You looked so funny! I don't think I've ever seen anything so funny. Cockroach, go and fetch the bike.'

Thomas's arm was given one final twist. Then the boy called Cockroach let him go and sauntered off to pick up the bicycle. He lifted it up and slammed it down roughly on its tyres, then vaulted onto the saddle as if he were doing a high jump, landing with an impact that made the whole bicycle shudder.

The other two roared with laughter. Thomas watched silently, rubbing his throbbing arm and wrists and trying not to let the tears of pain and helplessness spill over. His bicycle wouldn't last long in these rough hands; he could see that already.

Cockroach had backed up to the further end of the long alleyway, so that he was facing onto its downward tilt. Making loud revving noises, he crouched low over the handlebars and rolled the bicycle back and forth on the spot, as if warming up.

'Watch this!' he called boastfully and shoved off hard.

The bicycle shot forward in a blur of coloured wheels. Cockroach was a much bolder rider than the skinny boy had been. Pedalling furiously, he sent the bicycle flying towards the watching group, with far more speed than skill.

The bicycle was wobbling like a drunken thing under his unsteady hands. Then, suddenly, it began to zig zag, whipping from one side of the alleyway to the other, shaving the narrow walls so closely it made the watchers wince.

Cockroach was looking distinctly alarmed.

'Hey!' he shouted, 'What's going on?'

'You're going too fast, you Stupid!' yelled the big boy.

'Slow down! Slow down! You'll crash!'

'I can't! I can't!' wailed Cockroach. 'There's no . . .'

'Watch out!' cried the skinny boy. 'There's a pole – you're going to hit the pole!'

'Use your *brakes!*' roared the big boy and

the skinny boy together. But it was too late.

There was a sickening sound of impact. Cockroach's head and the wooden pole collided with a force that knocked him clear off the saddle. He landed hard, in a sprawl of out-flung limbs, and lay unmoving. The bicycle sank to rest beside him with a whisper of wheels.

For long seconds nobody moved.

'Cockroach! Are you dead, Cockroach?' whispered the skinny boy hoarsely. He hurried over to his friend and shook him urgently. After a moment, there was a whimpering sound. Cockroach raised himself slowly, both palms pressed to his forehead.

'There was no brakes,' he snivelled. Tears were coming out of his eyes. 'And the steering wouldn't work. I couldn't do nothing!'

'There's nothing wrong with the steering,' said the big boy. 'Or the brakes.'

He was busy inspecting the bicycle, wobbling its wheels about this way and that way, turning it round in circles.

'The bicycle works fine. I think you just can't ride.'

And now *he* climbed on, looking

confident and cocky.

Thomas watched expectantly, stealing forward so that he could have a better view. His arm and his wrists had magically stopped hurting, and he was suddenly feeling much more cheerful. He had to keep his hand in front of his mouth, in case the others happened to glance his way and catch him giggling.

He knew, of course, why the boys were having so much trouble trying to ride his bicycle! And he was filled with secret glee. Now it was the big boy's turn; Thomas could hardly wait to see what the bicycle had in store for him!

Cockroach and the skinny boy stood leaning together against the wooden pole, the one nursing his bruised bottom, the other his head. They too waited expectantly, watching the big boy closely as he pedalled past them.

But he was having no trouble that they could see. Smoothly he glided to the far end of the alleyway, swept round with a flourish and came sailing back again. The bicycle behaved itself beautifully with him. Clearly, there was not the slightest thing wrong with the steering – or any part of it.

'See?' the big boy grinned triumphantly, as he drew level with them again. 'No problem! You just have to know how to ride.' And he was off again; this time, pedalling out of the alleyway altogether, making a right turn into the street that ran past, adjacent to it. There, he halted for an instant.

'Catch you two at the bottom,' he called to his friends. And he was gone.

Grumbling, the other boys collected their yellow bags and trudged off after him. Thomas, they ignored as if he weren't there.

He stood too stunned to move, staring at the spot where his bicycle had disappeared. He simply couldn't believe it; his bicycle was gone – it truly was! The big boy had taken it; and he wasn't coming back again.

His eyes swam with tears. The figures moving up to the corner dissolved in a watery blur. By the time he had blinked his eyes clear again, the alley and the street beyond were empty.

He sat down on the greasy tarmac and put his head in his hands. His beautiful bicycle was gone! He would never see it again! He couldn't even bear to think of it in the hands of those *izigebengu*. They wouldn't care for it the way he had. They would treat it roughly, they would dent it and bash it about; scratch the lovely paintwork.

How could he have let them take it away from him like that? He should have fought them. He should have screamed for help. He should have done *something*.

A sound of commotion broke suddenly into his miserable thoughts. From the street beyond the alleyway, came yells and shouts and cries of panic. Thomas leapt to his feet and ran to the corner to see what was going on.

Racing towards him down the road, were two frantic brown figures – running as if the devil was after them. They dived into the entrance of the alleyway and cowered there, clutching at each other.

A second later, a red-blue demon of a thing burst into view and went hurtling, like the speed of light, past where Thomas stood. He caught one flashing glimpse of the big boy's face; he didn't look happy. No, not at all. His cheeks were the colour of grey ash. His eyes bulged like peeled litchis, and his mouth was stretched open into an ugly snarl.

'Aaaaieee!' he screamed, as the bicycle

sped like a missile towards the end of the street. It was clear that he had no control whatsoever over its crazy motion. It was a miracle that he was still on it at all. He was hunched over himself in strange contortion, his arms wrapped round the springs of the saddle, his toes twined together round the steering column and his knees somewhere near his ears. His bottom bounced wildly about in mid-air, slamming with painful thumps between the saddle's edge and the rim of the back wheel.

The bicycle reached the bend in the road and swerved round on itself in a smoking squeal of wheels – so low that the big boy's ear almost grazed the ground.

He screamed again, his eyes rolling like a mad dog's, and yet again, as the bicycle continued to swerve, spinning round on itself like a drunken top, faster and faster, making the watchers seasick just to see it.

The big boy wasn't screaming any more. Now he was very, very quiet. They saw him as a blurred brown blob at the centre of a spinning hurricane of red and blue. And then abruptly he was flung out. He flew through the air and crash-landed with a painful-sounding *whump*. It was fortunate for him that there was grass to soften his fall, or he would have broken bones for sure.

Slowly the bicycle unwound itself. Riderless, it wobbled over to where Thomas stood and leaned its weight against his legs like an affectionate dog.

Cockroach and the skinny boy were rigid with fright and astonishment. They squeaked like mice, babbling about witchcraft and *utokoloshe* they took to their heels and fled down the alleyway.

The big boy was busy being violently sick on the grass. Groaning like a dying man, he struggled at last to his feet and staggered off into the distance, stopping every now and then so that he could retch again.

Thomas slowly shook himself out of his daze. He looked down at the bicycle, now resting quietly against his legs, and was not sure whether to laugh or cry.

He fell to his knees, and hugged his arms tightly around the precious machine, burying his face into the soft leather of the saddle.

'Oh my bicycle!' he whispered fiercely, 'I thought I'd lost you!'

He heard a soft, silvery, tinkly sound. It might have been simply that his elbow nudged the bell by accident. But he could have sworn the sound was laughter.

TROUBLE WITH THE POLICE

The next morning, when Thomas's mother rose to go to her work at the usual time, she was surprised to find her son still sleeping beside her, instead of out and about on his usual early morning wanderings. And the morning after that, it was the same.

The truth was, Thomas didn't dare to venture out on his dawn rides anymore. The close brush with the bad boys had given him the fright of his life. Thanks to his bicycle, nothing serious had come of it, but the next time, they might not be so lucky.

Next time, it might be real *tsotsis* who tried to take his bicycle away from him, or the police who saw him and stopped him. He just didn't feel safe taking his bicycle into the street anymore.

But he missed those early morning outings terribly, and he knew his bicycle did too. It made him very sad, when he went to visit it in its secret place behind the kia, to see it standing there all lonely and neglected. It seemed to have lost much of its gleam and brightness. Its colours were dull. There was mud on its wheel-rims, smudgy finger-marks and streaks of dirt all over its frame. He spat on the side of his hand and tried to rub some of the grime away. But that only smudged it worse. What it needed, he decided, was a good clean – a proper wash and polish – it would make them both feel better.

He waited until the lunch hour, when he had the house to himself. His mother was off visiting some of her friends, and the Madam was out too. He fetched a bucket from the garage, some old rags, some water, and a teaspoonful of the liquid that the Master used for cleaning his car. He set everything out on the small patch of grass near the side of the kia, then brought the bicycle out of its gloomy den.

It seemed to perk up at once in the sunshine. He laid it down on the grass and set happily to work; wetting, wiping and rubbing, rinsing and polishing.

It was hot work, under the afternoon sun, but he didn't mind. He was enjoying himself, squatting on the green grass, watching his bicycle come to life again, as the grime dissolved under his hands and it regained its old sparkle.

He sang softly as he worked, a simple, repetitive song – the kind that sets the mind free to wander while giving the hands a rhythm to work by. He wasn't worried about keeping an ear open for unexpected callers. No one was likely to creep up on him without him knowing it. If his mother returned, he would hear her soon enough, slip-slapping up the side of the house long before she saw him. And if the Madam came back, he would hear the car. So he felt perfectly safe, working away like that right out in the open, he had forgotten about the neighbours.

In the big, two-storey house next door, the upstairs curtains twitched. And at the window, there appeared the cross, creased face of Mrs Grumper.

Mrs Grumper was always making trouble. Everybody in the neighbourhood knew how she loved complaining. If somebody played their music too loudly at night, she would call the police. If somebody's dog wandered into her garden, she would call the SPCA. If somebody's tree dared to grow leaning even the slightest little bit over on to her property, she would make them cut it down.

The first thing she had done when she found out that Thomas had come to stay next door, was telephone the Madam and complain. She didn't think domestics should be encouraged to bring their children into white areas. She was one of those who believed that blacks should stick to their own places.

And it made her crosser than ever now to look out of her window and see Thomas happily squatting on the green lawn – where, in her opinion, he had no right at all to be. What was more, his singing, soft as it was, had drifted up to her window and disturbed her afternoon nap.

She was just about to lean out and bark down at him to 'stop that noise this instant!' when her sharp eyes caught sight of what he was busy with.

Thomas had done a good job on his bicycle. Every spoke, every bolt, every inch of it had been polished till it shone. From wheel to wheel it gleamed like gold, sparkling so brightly in the sunshine that it hurt the eye to look at it.

Mrs Grumper's thin mouth set into an even thinner line. Her eyebrows almost met in the middle with the grimness of her frown. She didn't need anyone to tell *her* that the bicycle was stolen! Indeed, it never even entered her head that it might be honestly come by.

The only thing Mrs Grumper knew about black people was what she had read about them in the crime reports of the newspaper. She had never tried to get to know a black person herself, or even spoken to one – as one human being to another. She couldn't be expected to understand that there are good and bad black people, just as there are good and bad white people.

To her mind, *they* were all criminals. Thievery came as naturally to *them* as breathing. A lot of bicycles had gone missing from the neighbourhood during the past month or two. It was quite obvious to her that this was one of them. Fortunately, she thought, she knew her duty. The people of this neighbourhood were lucky indeed to have someone of her character living in their midst.

Ducking quickly back from the window, in case Thomas should look up and see he was being observed, she twitched the curtains back into place and hurried off to phone the police.

Since the bicycle looked so fine when he had finished with it, Thomas felt reluctant to put it straight back into its gloomy prison. He thought that he would leave it where it was for a short while, enjoying the free air and sunshine. He positioned it against the stem of a wild banana tree, draped some of the fat, concealing leaves across it – just in case – and went off to the garage to put his cleaning things away.

He was just coming out again, when he heard the heavy vibration of a large vehicle moving slowly up the street. He looked up curiously and felt the bottom drop out of his stomach.

Cruising up the road towards the house was a police van, a yellow one, with a blue star on the side-door and wire mesh covering the windows; the very sight of it was enough to strike cold dread into the heart of a young black boy.

There were many terrifying stories in the township about the police and what they did to black children. It didn't matter whether all the tales were true or not; the fear they inspired was real enough. And it was with ice in his veins that Thomas stood now and watched the big van creeping towards him.

He knew, he just *knew* that it had come for him. He willed it with all his might to keep on going, past the house. And for a moment, it almost seemed that it would. But then it appeared to change its mind and bounced to a stop, right opposite him. There were two policemen in it, a white one and a black. The black policeman leaned from the passenger window and called out;

'Hey you – boy – is this number 25?'

Dumbly Thomas nodded.

'You wait there. We're coming to talk to you.'

The police van backed up a little way and varoomed up to the top of the driveway, both policemen got out and came towards Thomas, looking immensely tall in their blue uniforms.

He looked up at them quaking, feeling faint with fear. He couldn't take his eyes off their gun holsters. Their faces were stern underneath the peaked caps.

'What is your name, boy?' barked the black policeman.

In a voice that was not above a whisper, Thomas told him.

'Do you live in this house?'

Yes, Thomas said, he lived here. That is, he was staying here for the holidays. With his mother. Who worked here.

The black policeman grunted.

'And is your mother home now?'

Thomas shook his head.

'And the Madam, is she here?'

'No, sir,' Thomas whispered, 'no one is here.'

'No matter,' the black policeman said. 'It's you we have business with anyway.'

He bent menacingly lower, his pointed cap shading Thomas's nose like an umbrella.

'Do you know why we should want to speak to you?'

Thomas pressed his lips together. Carefully, he shook his head.

'It's about the bicycle.'

Silence.

'The one you've got upstairs.'

'Have you got a bicycle upstairs?' the white policeman asked, speaking for the first time. His voice was not as stern as the black policeman's. He was younger – Afrikaans, Thomas could tell that from his accent. 'Boers,' they called them in the township; the Comrades spat the word out as if they were saying 'Enemy.'

Both policemen were waiting impatiently for Thomas to answer. He didn't dare to look at them. Should he lie, he wondered, and say no, there was no bicycle? But they would probably search and find it anyway. He would only make it worse for himself if he lied.

Unhappily, he lifted his shoulders up and down again.

'Yes, Baas, I have a bicycle upstairs,' he whispered.

'Oh yes,' said the white policeman, in Afrikaans. 'And where did you get it? You'd better tell us.'

The black policeman tapped him on the head with a hard forefinger.

'We want to know which house you stole it from.'

'And who helped you. Are you part of a gang?'

'We know there's a gang working this area.'

'We want to know the names.'

'And what else you've stolen.'

'Are you hiding that upstairs as well?'

They were firing questions at him so rapidly that he couldn't even think. He could only stand with his mouth hanging open, shaking his head from side to side and feeling his heart sink lower with every word.

'Talk, man!' rapped the white policeman. 'Or we'll take you down to the station and make you talk. We don't have time to waste.'

'Baas,' stammered Thomas, 'I didn't steal nothing Baas. This bicycle is mine – my own,' he insisted, stabbing himself in the chest with his finger so there should be no doubt. 'It belongs to me.'

'Yours, you say,' said the black policeman in Zulu. 'Can you prove that it is yours? Did you buy it in the shop? Have you got a sales receipt to show us?'

Thomas twisted his hands together behind his back.

'No, sir, I did not buy it,' he said miserably.

The black policeman folded his arms across his chest.

'Then where did you get it from, this

bicycle that you say is yours? Did somebody give it to you. Can you take us to that person?'

Thomas was quiet. It was on the tip of his tongue to tell them about the old woman. But why get her into trouble too? It would do no good anyway, they still would not believe him. 'Nobody gave it to me, sir,' he mumbled reluctantly. 'I . . . I just found it.'

'Oh yes – you *found* it!' The white policeman managed to sound mocking and threatening at the same time. 'And where did you find it? In somebody's front garden, I suppose!'

'No, Baas! I did *not* steal it, Baas. This bicycle, I found in . . . in the bush . . . up there near the river . . . I can show Baas the place.'

The black policeman made a snorting sound. He clamped a large, hard hand over Thomas's head.

'Sgebengu! Do you think we are fools enough to believe such stories? We know the bicycle is stolen; take us to it now, or it will be the worse for you.'

He didn't give Thomas the chance to protest further, but marched him towards the sloping pathway that led round the side of the house. The white policeman followed behind them.

Down in the street, a whispering knot of onlookers had gathered, among them, some of the bicycle children. All agog, they watched as Thomas was marched off like a criminal between the two blue uniforms.

Thomas felt hot waves of shame flood over him. Would they still be standing there, he wondered miserably, when the policemen marched him back again and threw him into the van to take him off to the station?

He tried to imagine what it would be like in that wired-in enclosure; hot and airless and dingy and frightening. He wondered if he would be taken straight to the police station, or left to rattle around in the back of the van all afternoon while they picked up other prisoners.

He thought about his mother, coming home to find him not there, and someone telling her that he had been taken away by the police. What a shock it would be for her! Her heart would break. She had brought him here to the city to keep him out of trouble. How could he make her understand that it wasn't his fault?

But it was his fault, a little voice inside him whispered guiltily: if he hadn't deceived her, if he had confided in her from the first, this trouble might have been avoided.

It seemed an endless journey to the top of the house. The policemen trudged behind him without speaking, their heavy boots tramping like those of an army. On trembling legs, Thomas led them past the kia, to the small patch of lawn beyond. He pointed wordlessly at the banana tree, and stood back.

The black policeman ducked forward and peered into the nest of leaves. He went round the other side, and brought the bicycle out. Thomas kept his eyes on the ground, tracing patterns on the grass with his big toe. He didn't dare to steal so much as a glance at his beloved bicycle; he knew the tears would burst loose if he did.

The white policeman moved past him and walked forward to inspect what the other one held. There was an endless moment of silence. Then, a whirring of pedals and chains as the bicycle was put back into its hiding place.

The two policemen came back towards Thomas, the black one dusting his hands on his thigh. But it was the white policeman who spoke. 'So that's your bicycle, hey, naughty boy?' he said. There was a note in his voice that hadn't been there before; he almost sounded as if he were smiling.

'You found it, you say? In the bush near the river?'

Thomas barely managed to nod.

'And it didn't belong to anyone, you're quite certain about that?'

Thomas shook his head.

'Well then . . . I suppose it's all right. You can keep this bicycle of yours . . .'

Thomas looked up at him in amazement.

'. . . if you're sure you didn't steal it from anyone . . .'

'If it was just lying there in the bush, belonging to nobody,' the black policeman agreed. His large hand descended to Thomas's head again, but this time, it rested there gently, not painfully as before.

Thomas couldn't understand what was happening. He gaped at the two policemen, both of whom now, were smiling down at him – *smiling* – as though they were all the best of friends!

'Well,' said the white policeman, after a short pause, 'We must be off. Goodbye little naughty one. Keep out of trouble now.'

He went striding off towards the stairs. 'And don't go finding any more bicycles, you hear!' he called.

The black policeman clicked his heels together and raised his hand to his hat in mock salute.

'Sala kahle,' he said.

And they were gone, clattering briskly down the stairs, their voices drifting back to Thomas. He heard the white policeman muttering something about '. . . trouble-making old women, as if we don't have enough work to do . . .'

Then there was silence.

A few seconds later, came the sound of the police van starting up. It was only when he heard it roaring off down the street that Thomas dared to believe they had really gone.

He didn't know what to think – his brain was in a whirl of confusion. How could it be that they had left without him? How could it be that he was standing there still on the sunny lawn – instead of being carted off to the station to be locked behind bars? And had the policemen really told him he could *keep* his bicycle? It seemed like a dream.

He rolled his wondering eyes slowly round to the banana tree. An awful thought struck him suddenly, and he raced forward and whipped the concealing leaves apart.

No red gleam peeped at him in welcome from the shadows. Against the stem, where his bright bicycle should have been, he saw only a strange, bulky shadow. He touched it apprehensively, then hauled it out with a cry, staring in dismay. This wasn't his bicycle! This was somebody else's – the ugliest, most decrepit machine he had ever laid eyes on.

It was black and heavy and dismal, half of it eaten away by rust, its frame so bent and buckled that it looked as if someone had gone to work on it with a hammer. Bare springs poked through the torn leather of the saddle. One wheel had half the spokes snapped off; the other had been dented and battered completely out of shape.

Thomas wanted to weep. Who had played this trick on him? Who had stolen his bicycle from under his nose, and left this sorry specimen in its place?

No wonder that the police had said he could keep it! Even they could not suspect he had stolen this! Nobody who was not soft in the head would go to the trouble of stealing such a wreck as this! It looked as if it would need a miracle just to make it go at all.

He rolled it back and forth on the grass. It let out the most pathetic cacophony of squeaks and rattles he had ever heard. Glumly he flaked some of the rusted paint from its crossbar. It came away in great scabby patches, like diseased skin. In places, where his nail scratched deeper, he caught glimpses of something glittery peeping through.

Thomas stared at that curious glitter for a long time. Then he fetched a sharp stone and carefully scraped away, stripping every flake of rusted paint from the crossbar, exposing the bare metal that lay underneath.

Only when he had quite finished did he allow himself to stand back and look.

And there it was, looping, bright as hope, from one end of the crossbar to the other; the golden writing that he recognised so well, that said,

'Inyosi.'

'My bicycle!' Thomas whispered. 'You *are* my bicycle . . . aren't you?'

The rusted bell tinkled at him sweetly.

The dented handlebars inclined themselves towards him, as if inviting him to climb aboard. He swung himself cautiously onto the broken saddle. It welcomed his bottom like an old friend – as smooth and soft as it had always been. He couldn't feel the poking springs at all!

The battered wheels rolled effortlessly forward and their squeaking made a music on the grass;

'*Inyosi! Inyosi! Inyosi!*' they sang.

Three times in quick succession, Thomas pedalled round the wild banana tree. He could have whooped with joy. There was no doubt at all that this ugly old wreck was his bicycle. It had disguised itself, that was all, to save him from the police. Once again, it had come to his rescue.

A commotion from below warned him that his mother had returned. He could hear her, hurrying round the side of the house, exclaiming as she came.

'Thomas!' she was calling to him anxiously. 'Thomas – are you there? What has happened? What did the police want here? Are you all right?'

Thomas shot off his bicycle. He dragged it hurriedly over to the banana tree and was about to stuff it in among the leaves, when something occurred to him.

He straightened slowly and looked at the machine in his hands. A white grin blossomed suddenly on his dark face; there was no need for him to hide his bicycle away anymore. No one would bother to try to take this poor wreck away from him now! Besides – the police themselves had given him official permission to keep it!

Still grinning, he laid his bicycle down on the grass, right out in the sunshine, where anyone could see it. Then off he ran to explain to his mother the reason for the policemen's visit.

CHANGED FORTUNES

Thomas had not intended to tell his mother the true story of his bicycle and how he had come by it. Fearing she would not believe him, he had thought it best to say only that he had found the old broken machine lying in the bush. Once he started speaking however, his words took on their own shape. Into her wondering ears, he found himself pouring out everything – all about his meeting with the Old One, his journey to the Spirit Tree and all his adventures since.

At first, he could see, his mother did not altogether believe him. But when he took her out onto the lawn and showed her the old bicycle lying there, when she saw his name, 'Inyosi' lit up in glittering letters on the dented black frame, her eyes grew very round.

'Hau! But this is a wonderful thing, my Thomas!' she exclaimed. She stared, a little doubtfully still, at the ancient thing lying there.

'And this bicycle, you say, was not old like this when you found it, but new and nice-looking?'

Thomas nodded eagerly. In loving detail he described to her for the second time its red and blue glory, its perfect, shining lines, its light, swift wheels. As he talked, he began to grow a little wistful. It was hard to remember what his bicycle had been – that dazzling machine that had looked so fine and made him so proud – and not long, just a little bit, to have it back again.

'I wish you had seen it, Mama,' he could not help saying. 'It was a *beautiful* bicycle – *very* beautiful.' A sigh escaped him. Then, lest the feelings of his present unlovely machine be hurt by such comparisons, he quickly said, 'But I don't mind so much that it is changed now.' He nudged a misshapen wheel fondly with his toe. 'It is still my special bicycle *inside*. It doesn't matter that it looks old and broken, and not very beautiful anymore.'

His mother looked at him for a long time without speaking. Then she put her arms around him and hugged him tightly.

'No,' she said softly, 'it doesn't matter. Those things, they matter only to people who don't know anything, who look with empty eyes, who see only the outside of things. Those kind of people,' she went on slowly, 'they look at a black boy like you, and they see only that he is black, not that there is gold inside him. They think that because he is black, he is worth nothing, that he must live only in a poor place and have only poor things, and not ride on beautiful bicycles, like white children do.'

She looked up at the windows of the neighbouring house as she said that, and her look was full of anger.

'They have stone in their hearts, those people! They make trouble for us all the time. They say, "Black people mustn't go here. Black people mustn't do this. They must leave their children behind them and come to work in the white houses."' Thomas had never heard her speak so fiercely. 'But what those people say will not matter anymore!' she went on. 'Everything is changing now. One day, soon, we will have our freedom. One day, it will not be necessary anymore for black children to live far apart from their mothers. One day, black boys like you will be able to ride their beautiful bicycles wherever they want to, without worrying about people making trouble for them. Maybe then,' she said, smiling at him, 'your bicycle will change itself back again. For it is a clever thing, this special bicycle of yours. It has a little of the Old One's wisdom in it, I think. It knows the right time for things.'

Thomas and his old black bicycle became a familiar sight in the streets of the neighbourhood. It made people smile to see them go by – the small black boy and his ugly, ancient machine that looked as if it ran on prayer and hope alone.

The bicycle liked to act the part. When there was an audience, it would behave at its most decrepit – all wobbly wheels and shaky steering – squeaking and wheezing and groaning as if the last life was being squeezed from it. But when they were alone, it sailed along without a murmur, smooth and silent as flight.

Now that they no longer had to worry

about being seen, they could ride whenever they wanted to. But their favourite time was still the early morning, when the city lay about them like a dreaming ghost, waiting for dawn, and the streets belonged only to them.

Later, when the sun rose, the enchantment would be lost. The streets would fill with traffic. And Silverton would become once more the world of the white people, where black boys did not belong.

Still, Thomas enjoyed the new freedom. It was nice to be able to ride about openly in daylight, in full view of all; to be able to mingle with the bicycle children as equals, mounted on wheels of his own.

He had hoped that having his own bicycle would make them friendlier towards him. But they ignored him as they always had. Sometimes, as he rattled past them on his shaking, squeaking machine, he would see them whispering together, giggling at him behind their hands. Then, he would long to show them; he would wish more than anything that he could have his bicycle changed back again.

In his imagination, he would see himself, seated on the red and blue wonder, parading before the white children's astonished eyes. He would picture them crowding round, hear their admiring gasps as he performed for them feats of skill and daring that not even Kevin could match.

But it was really only his pride that wanted to impress them. Once, he had longed to win the friendship of these bicycle children; now, he no longer cared.

The group had changed since earlier days. Its numbers had dwindled, and it seemed much less happy. Whenever Thomas saw them, they seemed to be squabbling. They spent a lot of time circling aimlessly around in the street, doing nothing in particular, looking bored and fed up with each other. Perhaps it was because they had lost their captain; for some reason Kevin was no longer part of the daily gatherings.

Thomas wondered often what had become of him. He never saw him these days, pedalling madly past with his daredevil grin and his fingers waggling in greeting or sweeping round the corners like a water-skier, with such style and skill that you wanted to cheer.

The neighbourhood seemed emptier for his absence. Thomas assumed that Kevin must have gone away on holiday somewhere – and he was sorry, for he was dying to show off his new riding skills to him. This white boy, he felt sure, would not laugh at his bicycle the way the other children did. He would recognise at once that it was a unique machine; he would appreciate its special qualities as no one else could.

He kept an eye out for him all the time as he rode about the neighbourhood, hoping he would reappear before the holidays ran out and the time came for Thomas to return to the township.

Once or twice, he thought he caught sight of him in the distance. But by the time he had pedalled over, the boy had disappeared. Anyway, he was sure he must have been mistaken. For the boy he saw was on foot, and Kevin, he knew, seldom went anywhere without his bicycle.

And then one morning, early still, as Thomas was turning out of the driveway for a quick ride before breakfast, he saw Kevin walking by on the other side of the road, looking very gloomy, with his shoulders hunched up to his ears and his hands thrust deep into his pockets.

He nodded to Thomas without smiling,

and his eyes fell wistfully on the old bicycle for a moment, before sliding quickly away.

Thomas hesitated, then quickly called out,

'Hey!'

And when the other boy glanced back, said, 'Where is your bicycle?'

He was answered by a shrug.

'Haven't got it anymore.' Kevin tried to sound as if he didn't care much. But his face said that he cared a lot.

'Had to give it back to the shop. It wasn't properly paid for.'

He kicked viciously at a stone.

'My pa lost his job.'

'I'm sorry,' said Thomas. And meant it. He knew what it was like to be the child of a parent with no job.

Kevin shrugged again.

'We'll be moving from here soon. Going to live in a *flat*!' he said disgustedly. 'With my grandparents, till my pa gets another job. They're pretty old,' he added glumly.

Thomas nodded. 'I live with my grandmother,' he said. 'She's old too.'

The other boy seemed to look at him properly for the first time.

'What's your name?' he asked abruptly.

'Thomas.'

'Mine's Kevin. How old are you?'

'Ten.'

'I'm eleven.'

They stood in silence, looking at each other awkwardly, the street between them.

'Do you want to ride my bicycle?' asked Thomas suddenly, all in a rush.

Kevin's face lit up for a moment. Then, 'That thing?' he asked dubiously. 'Does it go?'

'Oh yes!' replied Thomas, grinning, 'Yes, it goes!'

He crossed the road to where Kevin stood, the bicycle limping along beside him in a clatter of dragging chains and scraping wheels, putting on a great show of decrepitude for Kevin's benefit.

The white boy winced to hear the pitiful sounds.

'But how do you ride it!' he exclaimed, casting his practised eyes over the pathetic thing.

'The one wheel's got hardly any spokes and the other's all squashed . . . the chain's out of alignment and the handlebars are skew and . . . holy-moly! Do you actually *sit* on that saddle?'

Thomas started to say something, but then shut his mouth and merely offered the handlebars to Kevin in silence, hiding his smile.

The white boy took them with a shrug and swung himself gingerly onto the saddle.

'Funny, you don't feel the springs,' he admitted, squirming about on the broken leather. 'And the pedals go round OK. I suppose the brakes don't work too good, but . . . who really cares!' He grinned and the old daredevil light shone green in his eyes. 'Okey-dokey,' he said. 'Here goes nothing!'

With a mocking salute, he shoved himself forward and rolled noisily off along the street, soon disappearing round the corner. Thomas listened till the sound of squeaking and scraping had faded into the distance. Then he sat down on the soft grass to wait for their return.

The leaves of a young pawpaw tree sheltered him with soft shade. The morning swayed about him in its tones of green and gold. Peaceful sounds floated from the houses – the tunes of caged birds and drifting music, mingling with the drowsy hum of vacuum cleaners and floor polishers and washing machines.

Through the drawn-back curtains, he could see his mother, padding quietly about at her duties, looking young as a school-girl in her pink uniform and headscarf. The Madam appeared at the bedroom window in her dressing gown, waved briefly to Thomas, and then withdrew.

He sat for a long time in the street, patiently waiting. But Kevin and his bicycle did not come back. Presently, he began to grow anxious.

He wondered if he should have warned the other boy that this was no ordinary machine that he was riding. What if his bicycle was misbehaving itself with him? What if it was giving him the very same treatment it had given the *izigebengu* boys! He couldn't even be sure that it would allow anybody but himself to ride it at all.

Thomas pictured Kevin, lying hurt and helpless in some busy road. He pictured his bicycle, abandoned in some far away street, where he would never find it again. He jumped to his feet and began to pace restlessly, trying to decide whether he should go in search of them or not.

And then, to his relief, he heard a familiar

whoop. There they were at last, careering round the corner, swooping past in a shower of wind and wheels.

Kevin was crouched close over the handlebars, his hair sticking up like blond straw, his pale face flushed with laughter and delight.

'Hey!' he was yelling. 'Hey, Thomas – *what* a bicycle! Holy-moly, Thomas – is it *magical*!'

Thomas watched his friend whirl around the cul-de-sac, and glide to a perfect, whispering stop by his side.

'Yes,' he smiled. 'I know!'

Annie Dalton

THE WITCH ROSE

Laurel Fair didn't go into the garden looking for
trouble. She was just trying to find something
interesting for the class nature table . . . Then she saw
the witch rose.

Witch roses come secretly, and they mean trouble . . .
Laurel wanted more than anything to live happily in
the ordinary world with Mum and Baby Nina . . .

Can her wish come true?

'An exquisite blend of fantasy and reality'
Susan Hill, Sunday Times

Jamila Gavin

THREE INDIAN PRINCESSES

The stories of Savitri, Damayanti and Sita

* Savitri *

Savitri leaves the palace to live with her husband in the jungle. She carries a dark secret. Satyvan will die within a year . . .

* Damayanti *

Everyone wishes to marry Princess Damayanti, even the gods. However, even the gods consent to the virtuous princess's marriage to King Nala . . . that is all except a demon who lays a curse on the couple.

* Sita *

Prince Rama is about to become king when he is banished by his jealous stepmother for 14 years. His wife, the loyal Sita, follows, but this is only the beginning of their suffering . . .

Three vibrant and powerful Indian folk-tales retold with great sensitivity and charm.

Grace Hallworth

LISTEN TO THIS STORY

Brer Anansi and Brer Snake and *How trouble made the monkey eat pepper* are just two of the delightful stories included in this collection of West Indian folk tales.

Grace Hallworth has retold them with all the humour and vitality of expression which she herself enjoyed so much as a child in Trinidad – and she has even contributed her own magical version of why the Kiskadee bird is so called.

These stories are guaranteed to captivate children of all ages.

Also by Grace Hallworth

Mouth Open, Story Jump Out

Geraldine Kaye

COMFORT HERSELF

Comfort loved her mum; everybody loved Margaret. When the tragedy struck it was impossible to believe. But Comfort was on her own now.

'You have to stand up for yourself,' Margaret had said. And Comfort knew she had a choice. She could stay safe in England with her old-fashioned grand-parents – or she could try and go to her father in Ghana. It was a hard choice to make, and one she would have to go on making, in one way or another, for the rest of her life.

GREAT COMFORT, the sequel to COMFORT HERSELF, is also available from Mammoth.

Alison Prince

THE GHOST WITHIN

A ghostly trumpet . . . a lost photograph of a lost lover . . . blood on a dressmaker's pin . . . flowers of the dead . . .

Alison Prince has created a haunting collection of stories with the power to startle, disturb and alarm; they linger long afterwards in the shadowy corners of the reader's mind.

'A strong and compelling book . . .'
British Book News

'An excellent collection of imaginative, haunting stories . . .' *Financial Times*

Gillian Rubinstein

MELANIE AND THE NIGHT ANIMAL

Some people think eight-year-old Melanie is timid and shy – but she isn't really. It just takes her time to get used to new situations and new people, so moving house, starting a new school and trying to make new friends is a daunting prospect. But, in time, Melanie confronts her fears, makes friends with the boys next door and with Jasmine Hardcastle – Melanie even stays in the tent all night alone, waiting to see the mysterious night animal . . .

Set in Australia, this is a gentle and perceptive book about facing fears and making new friends.

Catherine Sefton

THE SLEEPERS ON THE HILL

'I wasn't afraid . . . not *really* afraid . . .'

It was young Tom Connor who discovered the strange bangle and its owner, Kate, who was even stranger. Kate wouldn't say where the bangle came from, but Tom had his suspicions – and they increased as more and more trouble came upon the people of Ten Cottages. None of the local villagers would have dared to climb Sleepers' Hill, let alone take anything from the ancient graves beneath . . .

Laura Ingalls Wilder

LITTLE HOUSE IN THE BIG WOODS

A true and exciting story of life in a log cabin on the edge of the Wisconsin Woods in the days of pioneering when Indians still threatened and life was full of adventure.

Anything could happen to one small family, with uninhabited country stretching away for mile upon mile in every direction, with bears and panthers lurking in the woods – but within the cabin there was gaiety, warmth, security, a sense of purpose and achievement.

This is the first in Laura Ingalls Wilder's trilogy about her family. The sequels, LITTLE HOUSE ON THE PRAIRIE and ON THE BANKS OF PLUM CREEK are also available from Mammoth.

A Selected List of Fiction from Mammoth

While every effort is made to keep prices low, it is sometimes necessary to increase prices at short notice. Mandarin Paperbacks reserves the right to show new retail prices on covers which may differ from those previously advertised in the text or elsewhere.

The prices shown below were correct at the time of going to press.

☐	7497 0978 2	**Trial of Anna Cotman**	Vivien Alcock	£2.50
☐	7497 0712 7	**Under the Enchanter**	Nina Beachcroft	£2.50
☐	7497 0106 4	**Rescuing Gloria**	Gillian Cross	£2.50
☐	7497 0035 1	**The Animals of Farthing Wood**	Colin Dann	£3.50
☐	7497 0613 9	**The Cuckoo Plant**	Adam Ford	£3.50
☐	7497 0443 8	**Fast From the Gate**	Michael Hardcastle	£1.99
☐	7497 0136 6	**I Am David**	Anne Holm	£2.99
☐	7497 0295 8	**First Term**	Mary Hooper	£2.99
☐	7497 0033 5	**Lives of Christopher Chant**	Diana Wynne Jones	£2.99
☐	7497 0601 5	**The Revenge of Samuel Stokes**	Penelope Lively	£2.99
☐	7497 0344 X	**The Haunting**	Margaret Mahy	£2.99
☐	7497 0537 X	**Why The Whales Came**	Michael Morpurgo	£2.99
☐	7497 0831 X	**The Snow Spider**	Jenny Nimmo	£2.99
☐	7497 0992 8	**My Friend Flicka**	Mary O'Hara	£2.99
☐	7497 0525 6	**The Message**	Judith O'Neill	£2.99
☐	7497 0410 1	**Space Demons**	Gillian Rubinstein	£2.50
☐	7497 0151 X	**The Flawed Glass**	Ian Strachan	£2.99

All these books are available at your bookshop or newsagent, or can be ordered direct from the publisher. Just tick the titles you want and fill in the form below.

Mandarin Paperbacks, Cash Sales Department, PO Box 11, Falmouth, Cornwall TR10 9EN.

Please send cheque or postal order, no currency, for purchase price quoted and allow the following for postage and packing:

UK including BFPO — £1.00 for the first book, 50p for the second and 30p for each additional book ordered to a maximum charge of £3.00.

Overseas including Eire — £2 for the first book, £1.00 for the second and 50p for each additional book thereafter.

NAME (Block letters) ....

ADDRESS ....

....

☐ I enclose my remittance for ....

☐ I wish to pay by Access/Visa Card Number

Expiry Date

Laura Ingalls Wilder

LITTLE HOUSE IN THE BIG WOODS

A true and exciting story of life in a log cabin on the edge of the Wisconsin Woods in the days of pioneering when Indians still threatened and life was full of adventure.

Anything could happen to one small family, with uninhabited country stretching away for mile upon mile in every direction, with bears and panthers lurking in the woods – but within the cabin there was gaiety, warmth, security, a sense of purpose and achievement.

This is the first in Laura Ingalls Wilder's trilogy about her family. The sequels, LITTLE HOUSE ON THE PRAIRIE and ON THE BANKS OF PLUM CREEK are also available from Mammoth.

A Selected List of Fiction from Mammoth

While every effort is made to keep prices low, it is sometimes necessary to increase prices at short notice. Mandarin Paperbacks reserves the right to show new retail prices on covers which may differ from those previously advertised in the text or elsewhere.

The prices shown below were correct at the time of going to press.

☐ 7497 0978 2	**Trial of Anna Cotman**	Vivien Alcock	£2.50
☐ 7497 0712 7	**Under the Enchanter**	Nina Beachcroft	£2.50
☐ 7497 0106 4	**Rescuing Gloria**	Gillian Cross	£2.50
☐ 7497 0035 1	**The Animals of Farthing Wood**	Colin Dann	£3.50
☐ 7497 0613 9	**The Cuckoo Plant**	Adam Ford	£3.50
☐ 7497 0443 8	**Fast From the Gate**	Michael Hardcastle	£1.99
☐ 7497 0136 6	**I Am David**	Anne Holm	£2.99
☐ 7497 0295 8	**First Term**	Mary Hooper	£2.99
☐ 7497 0033 5	**Lives of Christopher Chant**	Diana Wynne Jones	£2.99
☐ 7497 0601 5	**The Revenge of Samuel Stokes**	Penelope Lively	£2.99
☐ 7497 0344 X	**The Haunting**	Margaret Mahy	£2.99
☐ 7497 0537 X	**Why The Whales Came**	Michael Morpurgo	£2.99
☐ 7497 0831 X	**The Snow Spider**	Jenny Nimmo	£2.99
☐ 7497 0992 8	**My Friend Flicka**	Mary O'Hara	£2.99
☐ 7497 0525 6	**The Message**	Judith O'Neill	£2.99
☐ 7497 0410 1	**Space Demons**	Gillian Rubinstein	£2.50
☐ 7497 0151 X	**The Flawed Glass**	Ian Strachan	£2.99

All these books are available at your bookshop or newsagent, or can be ordered direct from the publisher. Just tick the titles you want and fill in the form below.

Mandarin Paperbacks, Cash Sales Department, PO Box 11, Falmouth, Cornwall TR10 9EN.

Please send cheque or postal order, no currency, for purchase price quoted and allow the following for postage and packing:

UK including BFPO — £1.00 for the first book, 50p for the second and 30p for each additional book ordered to a maximum charge of £3.00.

Overseas including Eire — £2 for the first book, £1.00 for the second and 50p for each additional book thereafter.

NAME (Block letters) ....

ADDRESS ....

....

☐ I enclose my remittance for ....

☐ I wish to pay by Access/Visa Card Number

Expiry Date